Night Time

Artemis Nyx

Published by East Anglian Press

Copyright © Artemis Nyx

The right of Artemis Nyx to be identified as author of this work has been asserted in accordance with the Copyright, Designs and Patents Act 1988.

British Library Cataloguing in Publication Data.
A CIP catalogue record for this book is available from the British Library.

ISBN: 978-1-9997117-6-4

Acknowledgements

Many thanks to the judges:

Poetry:
Helen Thwaites

Fiction:
Sandra Forder

Writing for Children:
Terry Tarbox

Front cover photo:
Richard Toombs

Cover creation by:
Suzan Collins

Front cover photographer:
KMorral

Editor:
Jo Wilde

Competition Winners

Poetry:
Kate Walsh
Fiction:
Pat Casselden
Writing for Children:
Marion Rainbird

Highly Commended

Poetry:
Neil Dench, Stuart Foulger, MJ Wells
Fiction:
Claire Walker, Janis Hall,
Natasha Mickleburgh

Commended

Poetry:
Karen JA Nunn, Diana Bettinson
Fiction:
Julian Cope, Rosalyn Whitfield,
Aisha Khalaf
Writing for Children:
Cara Mickleburgh

Introduction

Welcome to Night Time, our third anthology of competition winners. All the work featured in this book was entered in the 2017 East Anglian Festival of Culture writing competition, and every sale helps to raise money for Alzheimer's Research UK.

Between these covers you will find something for everyone. A lot of people have given generously of their time and talent, and you've done an amazing thing by buying it.

The winners are all here, along with other pieces the judges deemed to be of sufficiently high standard to be included. Once again, the bar was set very high, and the organisers were again thrilled by the response of writers to the competition.

Writing is by necessity a solitary occupation, and writers like feedback to help them feel connected to their readers, so please leave a review on Amazon.co.uk when you have read and enjoyed the book.

You, the reader, are supporting the vital work of a very worthwhile cause, as well as encouraging some new writers, and inspiring some established ones. Thank you.

Contents

Title	Author	Page
The Darkness of the Night	MJ Wells	1
The Secrets of the Night	MJ Wells	2
The Night Mare	Cara Mickleburgh	3
Night Time Reflection	NA Dench	10
A Room for the Night	Claire Walker	12
The Final Meeting Or, Parting Sorrow	Aisha Khalaf	19
Night Time Terror	Pat Casselden	24
Night Time	Rosalyn Whitfield	32
Frank Loved the Night	Rosalyn Whitfield	37
Night Time	Janis Hall	43
Night Time	Janis Hall	51
Night Time	Stuart Foulger	55
Moonbeam	Jeannie Abbot	57
Night Time	Julian Cope	65
Night Time (Soul & Heart)	Karen JA Nunn	73
Night Time (Just in Time)	Karen JA Nunn	75
Late Night Run	Natasha Mickleburgh	77
The Sounds of the Night	Diana Bettinson	84
Night Time	Marion Rainbird	86
Night Time	Kate Walsh	93

The Darkness of the Night

The darkness is upon me, now the sun has lost its glow.
It needs time to replenish, so for now it has to go.
The air has cooled to cast a chill round all it settles on,
And dampness seeps into my bones, now where did that come from?
I shudder, as my ears detect a rustling in the trees.
Enshrouded in the darkness, I've tripped, I'm on my knees!
My heart is pounding in my chest, my breath comes in short gasps.
My fear has taken over. Will this breath be my last?
And then it is upon me, as moonlight peeps through cloud.
The little dog that lives next door, all waggy-tailed and proud.

©MJ Wells

The Secrets of the Night

Darkness, all engulfing, enshrouding all it
meets. Enveloping, and permeating, with its
black velvet cloak.
Consuming the day and its optimistic beauty
with an ominous chill of fear, for what lies
beneath the cloak.
Suddenly, the moon presents itself from its
blanket of cloud,
It casts shadows and illuminates as one,
throwing silvery twinkles on the dewy field.
Its grass, subservient to its mastery of light and
shade, congruent to the breeze, softly shifting,
rippling, in its playful dalliance.
From the darkness of the trees, a hoot from an
owl breaks the anticipation, of what might be
waiting in the unknown depths, of mother
nature at her most secretive.
Snuffling, shuffling, movement from the
ground, unnerving, as imagination runs riot,
with the sounds of the unknown. Darkness
paralyses us with fear, yet
still it beckons, daring us to reveal the
mysteries it keeps hidden.
Cocooning us in sleepy, tranquil dreams.
Drowning us, in the torment of our
nightmares.

©MJ Wells

The Night Mare

Alice could feel the weight of Great Aunt Orla's gaze on her as she forced a thin smile on her face. Looking down at the old, worn horseshoe that nestled inside the bright pink tissue in her hands, she really tried not to feel disdain for it and for the woman who gifted it to her new baby daughter.

"It's…it's very…different…" she finally said, after struggling to find anything nice to say.

The woman in question gave Alice a wide toothy smile that was highlighted with far too much red lipstick. She spoke in a loud voice that sounded like she was on the verge of singing an opera.

"Of course it is! A lot of babes don't get one these days. It's a great shame as every new babe needs a horseshoe. It's traditional. Isn't that right Derek? Remember? I got you one when you were a wee lil' lad."

Derek, Alice's husband, briefly looked up at her from staring down at the baby girl in his arms. Ever since they brought the baby home, he made many excuses to hold her. Alice had to stop herself from laughing at his stricken face when it was time to put her back in her cot. Blinking, he nodded and replied.

"Yes, I remember, Auntie Orla. I think Mum might have thrown it away after a while because of the rust."

Orla tutted in response, the grey feathers bouncing on her floppy hat as she shook her head.

"Well, I wasn't going to give you a new one, now was I? Horseshoes are useless unless they have been well worn out. Your mother should know that."

Alice couldn't help a dismissive scoff escape from her lips at that.

"What is the difference? Surely a brand-new shoe looks better than a rusty one?"

She had also wanted to say that a horseshoe

wasn't even a good present for a baby but her eye caught Derek's as she spoke, seeing him silently begging her to stop. Alice ignored it and continued.

"And it would be a lot safer too, considering that he could have caught something horrible off it."

To her surprise, the older woman merely chuckled. Giving Derek a knowing glance, Aunt Orla turned her gaze back to Alice.

"Take it from me dear, it makes all the difference. Old, worn out horseshoes are the only way to stop the night mares coming into your room and eating your good dreams. They especially like children's dreams; why else do you think children try and tell you there is a monster in their rooms? It's because there is one, though they really can't hurt you; but they are a pest to get rid of."

Alice just rolled her eyes.

When Great Aunt Orla left an hour later, Alice had reluctantly taken the horseshoe upstairs after Derek had caught her about to drop it into the pedal bin.

"I know it sounds like superstitious nonsense

but Auntie Orla really believes in this stuff. It'll hurt her feelings if we threw it out. And it won't do any harm to the baby if we just hang it on the side of the cot, would it?" he said, smiling that dopey smile of his that Alice couldn't say no to.

However, she would be damned if that dirty piece of metal was going anywhere near her baby girl. Shoving the horseshoe right at the back of her bedside cabinet drawer, she figured that it would only see the light of day whenever Orla returned with that ghastly hat with the pigeon feathers stuck all over it.

***

Later that night, Alice woke with a start. Something was in their bedroom, padding softly on the carpet. She blinked in the darkness, thinking Derek had just gone to check on the baby in her cot at the end of their bed.

"Derek?" she whispered into the dark.

A soft snore came in reply. Quickly turning over, she saw Derek's sleeping form, his chest rising slowly against the covers. The padding became louder, the noise beginning to sound like hoofs. It sent a long cold finger trailing up her spine. Alice bolted upright in bed, her eyes darting around the room. Shadows of furniture that were harmless during the day now grew claws and fangs on the walls. Panic began to twist in her chest, squeezing her lungs. The sudden urge to check on her baby snapped her head towards the cot.

Alice almost screamed.

A large, black, horse-like thing stood close to the cot as its long neck bent over the railings. Its head hovered over where the baby was sleeping, making soft snuffling noises as its round nostrils inhaled her daughter's smell. Alice froze in horror, watching it swish its tail as it shuffled its hoofs to get closer to the cot. This couldn't be real! It had to be a nightmare! Suddenly, Great Aunt Orla's voice boomed in her head.

"Old, worn out horse shoes are the only way to stop the night mares coming into your room and eating your good dreams. They especially like children's dreams; why else do you think children try and tell you there is a monster in their rooms?"

The words snapped Alice out of her fear. Pulling herself out of the duvet covers, she wrenched open the drawer of the bedside cabinet. A whine left her mouth as her hands franticly threw everything out of the drawer in her search. She had to find it! She was so sure she put it in here! Where was it?!

A sudden thunk hit the side of the drawer. Alice let out a sob as she reached in towards the sound. Cool, rough metal scratched the palm of her hand as she clasped the horseshoe tightly. Pulling it out, she stood up, the soft carpet embracing the soles of her bare feet. Alice wobbled slightly as she took a step towards the night mare, holding the worn horseshoe out in front of her.

"Shoo! Go away!"

Even in her fear of the shadowy being, she couldn't help feel silly as she said those words. Yet it seemed to work. The black horse raised its head up at the yell, its ears pointing forwards. Glowing green eyes regarded her silently, watching her as she took another step towards it. Suddenly spotting the horseshoe in her hand, the night mare let out a loud squeal. It jumped back away from the cot, throwing its head up as it stomped its hoofs on the floor. Its actions gave Alice some confidence as she stepped closer, shouting,

"Get away from my baby!"

That seemed to scare the night mare; its

nostrils flared, letting out a frightened whinny. It quickly turned around and bolted, disappearing into thin air as it galloped away. Alice couldn't see which way it went nor of any traces of it ever being in the room. The bedroom seemed less dark now than before. Her arm slumped to her side, suddenly feeling like lead as she held the horseshoe loosely in her hand. She was shaking as she slowly walked to the cot, her eyes glancing around the room just to be sure they were safe. When her hand lightly grazed the cot's railings, she gazed down into it. Relief drained the tension in her body as she watched her daughter breathing quietly, unaware of what had happened above her.

Reaching down to stroke her daughter's soft cheek, Alice resolved to phone Great Aunt Orla to apologise and thank her for the wonderful gift in the morning. Derek might wonder about her sudden change of heart but she didn't think he would believe her if she told him the truth. He was still faintly snoring from the bed. How on earth did he sleep through her yelling? She'd never know. In the meantime, Alice would have to look in the kitchen for some string. She would need it if she wanted to hang the horse shoe on the cot tonight.

©Cara Mickleburgh

Night Time Reflection

Night Time, a quiet time, a time for quiet reflection.
As I lay here in my bed, my mind replays everything that happened this day.
I think of what was, what is and what may be in this time of quiet reflection.
In this time of quiet reflection, I dream of future greatness.
I wonder what the future holds as I lie here in my bed.
Can I be more than I am in this time of quiet reflection?

In this time of quiet reflection, I close my eyes and dream.
I dream of our time together as I look upon your face.
To know you're here beside me makes my life complete.
In this time of quiet reflection, the night's shadows dance around me.
They've been my long-time companions as I lie here in my bed.
Knowing they'll protect me means I sleep content.

In this time of quiet reflection, I know my night must end.
From this time of quiet reflection, I know what

I must do.
I stride forward from the night into this new
day to begin a new day's journey.

Oh, the night time, the quiet time, my time for
quiet reflection.

©NA Dench

A Room for the Night

I've been trying to ignore the noise for hours. Music, though not any kind of music I've ever heard before, and howls of laughter that are high, wild, a little hysterical. Do they know what time it is? Such a raucous din is not the kind of thing you'd expect a swanky hotel like this to condone. Swanky. That's a word Joe would use.

No. I'm not thinking about Joe. Joe's gone. He was waiting for me when I got home from work and I'd barely had time to put the kettle on when he just came out with it. That he's been seeing someone else, someone who, unlike me, understands his need for excitement and spontaneity. Then he threw his key down on the table and stalked to the door, flinging a parting shot over his shoulder - that I'm a boring mare and that I need to get a life.

Maybe he's right. I've never been a party animal like him. Come nine o'clock at night I'm more of a pyjamas-and-cocoa kind of girl.

Tomorrow will probably bring a world of pain and self-recrimination but right now, tonight, I'm just plain angry. That's why I'm here, maxing out my credit card. I just got in my car and drove, with no idea of where I was going

12

until I saw this place – a country house hotel, all eighteenth-century elegance. Without thinking I turned into the gravel driveway.

I booked myself into the most expensive room available. To spend the night in a posh hotel is on my bucket list, although I never anticipated that when it happened I would be spending the night alone. I've checked out all the facilities, including the quality of the complimentary biscuits and the expensive soap. The power shower was quite an experience, I have to say.

Afterwards, pink and exhausted, I settled down to have my own little pity party. I did something totally crazy and selected from the pillow menu just for the hell of it. I called room service. Sod the club sandwich; I ordered Chilean sea bass in Bordelaise sauce followed by a well-known brand of luxury ice cream – a whole pint of it, strawberry flavour. Not to mention the bottle of Prosecco.

And then the party really started. Theirs, not mine.

Now, I've had just about enough of lying here listening to other people having a good time. I fling myself out of bed and throw wide the window. The air is heavy with the perfume of night-scented flowers, and ghostly-pale roses are glowing in the moonlight. There's light spilling onto the lawns from above, a flickering, dancing light and I can see shadows flitting across it, jumping, writhing, twisting.

Odd, though - I can't hear a thing out here. The hair on the back of my neck stands on end as a small animal cry of fear pierces the darkness. Then silence once more. I shiver as I realise for the first time how remote this place is.

Back inside, the noise is as bad as ever, if not worse. I'm going up there to complain. I pull on my jeans but leave on my pink cotton nightie, the one with a sleeping kitten on the front, tucking it into my jeans. I pad along the corridor and up the stairs.

At the top it is pitch black but there's a glow at the end of the landing where light is seeping through a crack in the double doors. It feels almost as if I'm being drawn inexorably towards it and by something other than righteous anger. I slip into the room.

Into pandemonium. If the Rio carnival and an Ibiza rave had a love-child, this is what it would look like. Light from a thousand candles is bouncing off huge gilt-framed mirrors, reflecting and re-reflecting into infinity.

Glinting in coloured glass goblets and shimmering on bejewelled silks. A fire is blazing in a huge marble fireplace. And still the music, the strange, haunting music.

I hurl myself into the maelstrom and I am whirled away. Faces obscured by elaborate Venetian masks, expressionless and empty-eyed, turn my way as I press my way through the seething crush, my senses assailed from all sides by wafts of perfume and incense, musk and warm bodies.

"Who is in charge here?" I shout, but no one hears me above the pulse of the music and the voices and the laughter.

Then the crowd parts and there, at the eye of it all, I see him.

This guy is definitely in charge, it's obvious by the way people are fawning around him. He's too tall for me to tap him on the shoulder, so I touch his muscled, elaborately-tattooed arm. He's shirtless, his body glistening with a faint sheen of sweat. He has burnished, bronze-coloured hair. He turns, and although his face is partly obscured by a black silk mask I can see amber eyes glinting within. It's probably just the candlelight reflecting in them.

I open my mouth to complain but he reaches

15

out and places a finger on my lips.

He doesn't say anything, just holds out his hand so, unthinking, I take it and let myself be pulled into the heart of all that light and life and heat. He takes me on a waltzer-ride of sensation and I exult in the moment. Suddenly all I want is to be here, now. For this night to be all there is. To not be boring little me, just once, and to experience the excitement I find I have secretly craved all this time.

***

I wake to a bright dawn. To sunlight instead of darkness, birdsong instead of laughter - and to the realisation of how the whole numinous night has roused some slumbering thing within me that won't be easily soothed. I went into that room the dull creature Joe said I was, but I have emerged as someone else entirely. I stretch luxuriously and catch the scent of my own skin, redolent of smoke and incense and something ineffable but undeniably reminiscent of him.

Breakfast, I think. I'm ravenous.

I go downstairs, sans luggage, wearing yesterday's clothes and feeling like I'm doing the walk of shame. It feels marvellous.
"Who stayed on the top floor last night?" I ask

the receptionist.

He gives me the strangest look.

"No-one, Madam. The top floor has been abandoned for years. Not a soul has been up there since they blocked off the stairs after the fire."

"Fire?" I echo.

Part of me wants to tell him he's mistaken. The rest of me isn't liking the way this is going one little bit.

"Yes, the fire. Some lavish birthday celebration, apparently, where things got tragically out of hand. Several people died in the blaze, so I'm told."

Horror and horrible fascination are fighting a bloody battle inside me, along with an encroaching sensation of nausea.

"But there were people up there last night," I insist faintly. "I…um…heard them."

He raises a condescending eyebrow.

"Did Madam make use of the minibar last night, at all?"

He's squinting at the bill, clearly seeing that bottle of Prosecco I ordered.

"How dare – excuse me!"

A man is passing whose badge says Richard Stoker, Manager. He's tall, with bronze-coloured hair. With mesmerising, amber eyes. I lose my train of thought.

"Your receptionist needs customer service training," I manage to say.

I am ensnared by those eyes. Then I blink and realise I haven't heard his reply. There might have been an apology. Exclusive offer, I think he said, in a dark, smoky voice. Something about the Manager's Special. An invitation.

Is that look in his eyes saying what I think it is?

"Thank you," I say. "That would be…most acceptable. Do I need a ticket or something?"

"You know where to come," he says. "All you have to do is book a room for the night."

© Claire Walker

The Final Meeting Or, Parting Sorrow

As the full moon rose above the calm sea shedding a silvery grey light over the landscape, a figure swam towards the white sandy beach and slipped out of the warm tropical water.

Anyone looking would see the silhouette of a tall, well-proportioned female with long shimmering hair of indeterminate colour, swishing from side to side past her waist and creating a halo effect around her small, oval, face. The figure walked purposefully, with easy strides, towards the silent coconut grove, its trees casting ghostly shadows.

As she neared me I moved into the moonlight. She stopped, looking at me with large aquamarine eyes softened with the glow of...is it pride or love, I wonder? As I move towards her I see she is smiling and, yes, her eyes are glowing with love for me.

"You have come as promised," I said.
"I always keep my promises to you," she replied. "You should know that by now."

The sound of her voice never fails to thrill me. It caressed my ears like a warm southerly breeze and sounded akin to soft rain tapping gently on my bare flesh.

"I brought a cloak to cover your nakedness," I said, as I held it up and moved forward to put it on her shoulders, tiptoeing to do so. I scooped her thick, silvery tresses and placed it over the cloak, stepping back.

"You smell of salt, fresh seaweed and …something else. What is it? It's making me feel a little homesick."

She opened her arms and I walked into them feeling her soft flesh, warm and welcoming. I placed my face against her breast.

"I have missed you so," she whispered into my thick dark locks. "Come, let us sit a while. Our time together is short. Tell me how are you finding life here now? Are you happy?"

I thought for a moment before answering. "People here are, on the whole, good. They show love and care towards each other. It is not the same in all places on the earth. There are those who take pleasure in causing pain and distress to their fellows."

"Have you come across many such people?" she asked as she drew me closer to her.

"I avoid them when I can and when I cannot I confound them with tolerance."

She looked at me questioningly.

"By that I mean the worse their behaviour towards me, the more I respond with love and understanding. Others tend to respond to unkindness by becoming angry and giving like for like. I see no benefit in such action. Dislike, I find, begets dislike, and leads to discontentment and unhappiness which to me means being uncomfortable within myself. In such a state, I can neither rest nor enjoy anything, not even the blue of the sky or the brightly coloured birds that seem to fly around just for my pleasure."

As I stopped for breath she stroked my hair, and in her melodious voice asked me, "Are you ready to return?"

"I can no longer return. I will not fit into that world any more. I remember the calm, the peace, the pervading aura of constant love emanating from our species. That memory warms me when life here takes an unexpected turn. However, I thrive, even enjoy the challenges the earth people face; from each other and from the elements. It stimulates my mind and causes me to think deeply about actions and reactions and its effect on our existence."

"We passed that stage eons ago," she

responded softly. "I understand your fascination with the species but they are a dangerous race, unpredictable."

I stroked her brow, smoothing away the frown gathered there.

"That is the attraction. The uncertainty makes life and its pleasures all the keener."

"This is the last time your father, the King, will allow me to visit you. He says my thoughts cause shock waves and perturb the others in our world for some time after my return."

My face crumpled and large tears rolled down my cheeks. She touched them in astonishment.

"You have become one of them! I have not seen tears since I married your father."

"Mother, I shall miss your annual visits. I had no idea there was a limit to the number of times you could visit me."

"I do not want to cause you pain my child. I wanted you to be free to choose. Your father agreed to this when he married me, a woman of this world whose heart could no longer bear the poverty, senseless fighting, suffering and death of children and good people."

"Shh, shh, it is all right, mother. I am old enough now. Although never old enough to live without seeing you, I will manage. I have news. I have met a young man. He has a peaceful soul and a loving heart so I will not be alone. Will Father let you come to meet your grandchildren?"

"I know not but I shall ask. Be at peace. We can see you in spirit always. I will know if you need me. Come, the moon is waning. Walk with me to the water's edge."

We put our arms around each other and walked in unison to the azure blue-green waters of the Pacific Ocean. My mother turned towards me, kissed me tenderly on each cheek, handed me the deep red cloak and walked into the water to the craft awaiting her. I watched, experiencing the bitter sweet pain of parting as her transport lifted from the water and zoomed off into the night sky.

©Aisha Khalaf

Night Time Terror

I could feel the blood oozing from behind my finger nails as I scratched frantically on the damp, musty wood. The silence engulfed me. How long had I been here? If he thought I would lay down I die, he was mistaken. He didn't know me at all. The shimmer of light that had filtered through a small crack had now disappeared. Night time had taken over. Darkness was my greatest fear, but I knew I mustn't give in to it.

I took some deep breaths as the earie silence made me shiver. An owl hooted. Was that a glimmer of moonlight?

We had been communicating for several weeks before arranging to meet. He had seemed so nice, so kind. We appeared to have loads in common - good food and wine, countryside walks and a great love of animals. When I told him about my little dog Carrie, and our love of walking, he said he couldn't wait to join us.

"The woods are great near where I live. Your dog would love it."
"This place is lovely," I enthused on our first date. He had taken me to the best wine bar in town and we had talked all evening. Well I talked and he listened mostly. He didn't go on

about his exes as a lot of dates did, in fact he didn't talk about himself much at all.

"I must be boring you. Tell me a bit about yourself."
"My life is quite dull. I work in construction. Have never been married. I have my own house and have lived by myself for five years now. That's me in a nutshell. I'd much rather find out all about you."

Why did I think he was just being modest? Considerate even. I wasn't stupid. I've always prided myself on being a good judge of character but the alarm bells never even pinged. He asked questions that I freely answered, thinking how attentive he was.

Carrie liked him too - but I suppose Carrie liked anyone that gave her attention. Our following dates took in walking with her through the park, and nearby seashore, but her favourite place was the woods near his home, where she could dart in and out of the trees, chasing rabbits.

"I'm just not sure about him."

I had taken him for dinner to the home I shared with my mum. She wanted to meet this man who I had talked about non-stop recently. I thought it had gone well and he even took her flowers.

"I can't put my finger on it but he makes me a little uneasy. I'm probably wrong but just be careful."
"Oh, Mum. No one would be good enough, would they?" I gave her a hug. "He's OK. I'm a big girl now. Trust me."

It was three months into the relationship when I began to have doubts. It started with comments about me wearing makeup. He said he wasn't keen. Then he got upset when I wanted to go out with friends.

"But I had plans to take you out. I've got tickets for that film you said you wanted to see."

He sulked big time if I said no to him. At first, I thought it cute that he loved me so much, but eventually I had enough. He was stifling me.

"This isn't working. I really like you but I need more space."

He begged me to change my mind, but I stood firm and eventually he appeared to accept my decision. He even wished me well. It all went quiet or at least I thought it did.

The first time was after I'd been to the cinema with a friend one night. It was dark as I went to my car to find a note under my windscreen wiper.

'I still love you. I still want you. Please give us another chance.'

I quickly glanced around but there was no one around. Was he watching me now? How did he know where I was?

That was just the start. Whenever I went out at night he seemed to know my movements. I never saw him but I was convinced he was there. He didn't scare me though. He had never shown the slightest sign of violence or even raised his voice to me. It was just unnerving. I wanted him to leave me be.

"You should report him to the police," mum said. "It's only when it's dark at nights that he's stalking you. He's a coward clearly, but I'm worried for you."
"He's harmless, Mum. I hurt him, that's all. He'll soon get fed up."

It was only when he left a note saying he was going to kill himself that I first panicked. "Please just talk to me. I want to know what I did wrong. Just talk to me. You can say when and where we meet."

I felt a sense of guilt. Maybe I should, then he could move on and leave me alone.

"Please listen to me. The man's unstable."
"Oh, Mum, he just wants to talk and I need to convince him once and for all that it's over. Texts haven't worked. I need to see him face to face. He's just unhappy and it's my fault. I have to fix this."

It was daylight and the park was an open space where generally other people were about. He seemed calm and rational and Carrie was pleased to see him. I loved that soft side of him as he fussed Carrie and for a moment wished things hadn't changed between us. His hand rested on mine.

"You're looking good. Thanks for coming."
"Your last note scared me. I know we're over but I don't want anything bad to happen to you."
He looked genuinely upset. "I'm sorry. I shouldn't have done that but I miss you so much. Can't we try again?"

For a minute, I felt myself weaken. He wasn't a bad man. But memories of his behaviour kicked in. I mustn't weaken.
"It wouldn't work. I can't love you as you want

and you deserve someone who can."

It was then that his eyes grew dark. Calling Carrie to my side I quickly bent and attached her lead. As I looked up, I gasped as I saw something shiny pointing to my side. He was holding a knife.

"Do as I say and I won't hurt you."

Grabbing my arm, he marched us out of the park to his car, with Carrie trotting along beside me. Where was everyone? Bundling us into his car, he locked the doors and drove quickly away.

"This is silly. Please let me go. We can stay friends - talk about things and maybe even try again."
"Don't take me for a fool. You made your feelings perfectly clear. If I can't have you, no one will. Get out – now."

The dusk was beginning to fall and the temperature was dropping. I felt the knife in my side as he marched us into the woods. A freshly dug grave lay in front of me. I was aware of screaming not realising it was coming from me. I tried to run but he had a tight hold and the knife jabbed at my flesh.
"No - please no!"

But he was beyond reason. Carrie was yapping. Did she think this was a game?

It must have been several hours now. I could taste mildew from the wood and earth above and around. My throat hurt from yelling. My legs were numb. My life flashed before me. I had so much to live for. Why could mum see what I couldn't? It was so dark. So very dark. Wildlife scuttled and screeched around. The noises of the night time echoed all around.

I must have dozed before being suddenly aware of voices. I yelled. I tried to kick the lid but my legs wouldn't move. Barking. Footsteps. Shouting. Was I hallucinating? It all went silent. I screamed a piercing scream. Was this where I died?

Barking. Barking again - that was Carrie. I knew that was Carrie. I shouted her name. Silence. Then voices. What were they saying? Was that him out there? Was he waiting for me to shut up? I screamed louder. Damn him. "Rot in hell, you bastard."

"She's in there. My baby. Hurry. Please hurry." Was that mum? I wanted mum so badly. I'd never ignore her again.
"Hang in there. We'll get you out."

I wasn't dreaming. Carrie was yapping. The voices were becoming clearer. It was getting lighter.

In the safety of a hospital bed, my wounds were treated. Surrounded by nurses, doctors and police, I was safe, but I was too scared to even shut my eyes.

I was told he had taken his own life, but I felt no sympathy. He left me to die in terror. His suffering was over, but I couldn't see beyond my distress. Night time would forever remain my nightmare.

©Pat Casselden

Night Time

Being homeless wasn't much fun and I can't remember a lot of it but I'll tell you what I can recall.

The date I moved into my new home is forever etched into my brain. It was the third of January but I've no idea of the time. All I know is that it was very late at night and everyone had had their dinner although some had been saved for me.

These days, as I sit in a comfortable chair and gaze into the fire, I ponder on the mysteries of life. I wonder, you know, if it's because I'm black. I don't find this a problem but some people obviously do. I'm also a female and very slim so, slightly built female, black and with, even if I say so myself, the most gorgeous eyes. I know that other blacks sometimes have trouble with their colour but then so do whites. Every creed, colour, race, no matter where, there is usually someone saying they don't like them. Is that though a good enough reason for rejection? Maybe it's because I can be a bit aggressive at times and I'm the first to admit it. I'm fine if everything is going my way but I hate being told what to do, I don't like people invading my space and if anyone or anything annoys me, then I do tend to lash out.

Over the years foster homes were found for me and I used to get very excited and my spirits were raised that perhaps this time it would be permanent. My hopes were dashed, as I was rejected, not just once, but several times and I could never understand why no one wanted me and I always ended up back on the streets. After the third placement, I gave up trying to be nice and took to the streets again.

On reflection, I could have tried harder to get on with my foster parents and their children but a lot of them thought they had a right to invade my personal space and I had to do everything on their terms. I used to eat, when I had food, when I wanted and not at set times as they did and I slept when I wanted not when it was their bedtime.

You know, life on the streets wasn't always that bad, although the winter nights were obviously the worse. I was lucky in some ways, I had one thick coat, which, provided it didn't get too cold, was enough. It's best to travel light anyway; too many thieves out there.

I survived mainly due to the kindness of strangers who fed and watered me, not the good wholesome meals that I dreamed of, but their leftovers for which I was grateful. I remember I did get an awful lot of chicken and in the end, I refused to eat it. I refuse to drink milk as in my street days I got a lot of that as well. I suppose people were being kind and milk is supposed to be full of goodness but it wasn't for me.

Finding somewhere to keep warm and dry was another problem and I think I know every bus shelter, every hedgerow, and every used and disused shed in the district. Sometimes, when I was feeling particularly lonely I would look at houses, choose one and if the lights were on I'd peep in the window. If I liked the scene within, for example, fire lit, what bliss, heat, dinner being eaten, maybe scraps for me? Then I'd make my presence known. Mind you, it didn't work every time, as more often than not, the door would open and someone would scream at me to go away.

Sometimes I would be sent packing with a bit of food in my tummy, which wasn't too bad. Towards the end of my homeless days it was really easy to get a bed for the odd night or two, so easy in fact that I don't know why I didn't think of it before.

This method works better at night, works even better if it's raining, or better still if it's snowing. First of all, make sure you are so wet that the water is running off your coat and you are stood in a puddle. When the door opens, look even more pathetic than you feel, make some sort of noise and ask for a bit of food and a drink. Looking like a drowned rat seems to soften the hardest of hearts and once over the doorstep you've got it made. A word of warning though: once inside do not wander from room to room, do not touch their possessions, keep your nose out of cupboards and drawers and do not gulp down any food they offer you. You might be starving and you know that you haven't eaten for a week but if you eat too quickly you will be probably be sick. People who offer the hand of friendship do not like you throwing up on their carpets or on their expensive furniture.

Illness finished my homeless days, and I was found wandering the streets, thin, drawn and hardly able to walk, and to be honest I don't think I would have lasted much longer.

Once again, I was taken into care, but this time I was given my own room so I had my own space and was able to keep away from people I didn't like. I was given medical attention, lots of food, but really, not enough love. I stayed there for a few months and during that time I was fostered out several times but the same old problems occurred and I was rejected and put back into care.

Christmas came and went and then on the 3rd January I was finally adopted into a loving, caring home. I want for nothing as I am spoiled rotten and apart from some medical problems I am enjoying life to the full.

Time now to curl up in my favourite armchair and have forty winks before dinner. Before I doze off, I must give thanks to the cat's home for finding me my forever home and you know, being a much-adored cat is not that bad after all.

© Rosalyn Whitfield

Frank Loved the Night

Frank loved the night; always had. He worked all day on the farm and worked hard, so hard that he never had time to himself, never had time to sit and think.

He'd never needed a lot of sleep so once the last jobs had been done he'd sit under the indigo blue sky and gaze up at the stars. The night time was his time. A time for reflection and time to work out what to do next. Tonight, though, he was troubled, as he didn't know what was going to happen to his beloved farm.

The night was, for a change, relatively quiet. He couldn't see the moon or the shooting stars that meant so much to him. If only the clouds would clear, he thought. If he could see just one shooting star he knew everything would be all right. Shooting stars were good omens according to his parents.

All he could see were the tubes and drips snaking their way into his body. Bringing in the good and taking out the bad. The heart monitor beeped in its quiet steady way for which Frank was grateful. A couple of times it had flat lined but after a lot of effort from the medical team order was restored. Quiet footsteps padded past his door and muffled voices receded as the staff went about their work.

Frank settled down for another sleepless night and his mind drifted back down memory lane to when he was a young, fit farmer working the land with his brother Chris. He remembered that every night, no matter how tired he was, he herded the stock to safety. They were his main concern.

During difficult times Frank had slept out in the fields spreading his blanket on the dusty earth and watching as the sun slipped below the horizon, leaving the sky, for a few seconds, streaked with pink and blue before being plunged into total darkness. When the full moon rose, it bathed the landscape in its brilliance and nothing, not even the darkest corner, escaped its rays.

Frank shifted in his bed feeling confined by the starched sheets and the heavy blanket and wished he was back in the farmhouse. The house really needed extending but as he was on his own he was content with basic needs. Apart from that there was important work to be done on the farm and there was where his money went.

He raised cows and sheep and kept some hens

for personal use. He used to enjoy a breakfast of eggs as long as his girls did their bit. Even if they stopped laying, Frank would never get rid of them. Some fields were turned over to crops, some he sold, some he kept for the animals' winter food. He remembered with a smile the times in the early years when he'd slept near the animal pens. He could still hear the sheep bleating gently and the cows mooing softly as they settled for their night in the byre. The pigs made comical snuffling noises as they rooted around in the hay looking for morsels of food. The only sounds that reached his ears tonight were the sounds of the hospital.

The brothers had inherited the farm from their father and they had worked together to make it something that they could be proud of. Frank recalled the planning and planting of the crops; they had envisaged acres of golden wheat growing tall and strong and even more acres planted with corn. They had cut down of some of the trees and sawed the trunks into planks which they then dried and seasoned and used it to build the stables that housed their two horses.

The hen house came from a neighbour who no longer had any need for it. The orchard took a long time in the planning as neither brother could decide which variety of fruit to grow. In the end Frank made the decision and the orchard was now full of cherry trees.

A nurse quietly entered the room and checked the notes at the foot of his bed. Frank feigned sleep and carried on with his memories.

His brother Chris was married with two children, a boy, Barry, who was at Agricultural College, and a girl, Lucy. Lucy was the apple of her father's eye and beautiful like her mother Sue. When newly married, they had lived with Frank, but Sue was a city girl at heart, she didn't like living in the countryside, surrounded, she said, by nothing. They had moved back to the bright lights and hustle and bustle of the city although they did make the occasional visit to see Frank.

On marriage, Chris had handed over his share of the farm, livestock and outbuildings knowing full well that Frank would take great care of it. He was committed to it in a way that Chris never was. Frank hoped that his nephew, Barry, would carry on with the farm after his death but the boy politely declined the offer saying that he wanted to study husbandry. Finally sleep overcame Frank and he drifted off into a world full of cows, pigs and sheep.

The new day dawned with a sky so blue it

lifted the spirits. Frank had his breakfast of eggs and then settled down to rewrite his will wondering who could he ask to take over his beloved farm. Before he could put pen to paper a nurse popped her head around the door. "An early visitor for you, Frank," she announced, with her usual cheerful tone.

To Frank's surprise, in walked Barry, who he hadn't seen for a couple of years. Barry ran up to the bed waving a piece of paper at his uncle. "I've graduated from college," he said, the words tumbling out of his mouth in excitement "Please may I change my mind and work with you on the farm. I'm getting married and Emma and I love the countryside. With your permission, we would like to build a house and bring up any future children on your farm."

Frank smiled at the excitement that was emanating from his nephew and thought; he's just how I was at that age. Barry was even more excited when he found out that Frank had left him the farm in his will, not knowing that his uncle was seriously ill.

Barry left late in the evening full of dreams, plans and hope. Frank, happy and contented that his farm was safe in his nephew's keeping turned his gaze to the window and noticed that night had fallen. The moon was high, the stars sparkled and a shooting star sped its way across the heavens. A good omen for the farm, he thought, as his heart monitor slowed and then flatlined...for the last time.

© Rosalyn Whitfield

Night Time

The deck of the Albatross rose and fell gently, dark water rippling against her wooden hull.

Jonas felt the residual warmth of the sun through the wood as he lay perfectly still, staring at the sky. With the sun sinking over the horizon, odd pin pricks of light began to sparkle above him. Soon the inky blue blanket would be littered with millions of tiny flashes of silver. Nowhere else could you find the same kind of peace.

A noise below deck coaxed him out of his reverie. Sir John, dressed for dinner, tutted impatiently. Lady Caroline appeared behind him, checking her watch. They were late. Much younger than her husband, Jonas noticed how beautiful she looked with the rising moon behind her. In one fluid movement, he was on his feet and at her side, his wide smile telling her it was ok, she wouldn't be late and the twinkle in his eye, teasing her for worrying.

As the rowing boat moved steadily towards the shore, Jonas felt Sir John relax. The harbour lights were calling to him, away from the darkness, away from the silence of the rocking boat. He was not a natural sea creature.

Jonas left them at the water's edge and watched as they picked their way up the sandy beach, their shoes filling with the soft golden grains, still warm from the day's sun.

Jonas planted an oar silently into the water and turned the boat round towards the Albatross, swinging gently against her anchor, waiting for him, her...light twinkling against the black backdrop. Not for Jonas the busy marina where the Albatross would be forced to jostle among the playboy yachts or the harbour where she would be nudged by the fishing boats, sticking out from the walls like crooked teeth. Jonas valued his peace. Mullion cove was quiet and, at night, filled with the scents of bougainvillea and sweet jasmine drifting down from the gardens on the clifftop above.

He tied the boat up and swung himself silently on board. In the cabin, he checked his charts, plotting his course for when he would set sail again. It was a journey he had made many times but Jonas was meticulous in his preparation, checking and rechecking every detail.

The weather was set fair with enough wind to take him quickly. It was looking good. Lifting a cold beer from the galley, he padded barefoot to the bow and stretched out, his back against the mast. Darkness, now complete, brought with it a thousand sounds, all familiar and comforting. Jonas closed his eyes.

Moments later, a flashlight from the cliff path roused him. He remained still, watching the cliffs leading down to the cove, the high water concealing the caves. Another signal brought him to his feet and Jonas slipped quietly from the deck to the rowing boat.

Not a word passed between the two men as they transferred boxes from the cave to the boat. They worked in perfect tandem borne of years of practice. Finally, with the rowing boat sitting low in the water, Jonas turned again for the Albatross.

As the curtain of night pulled back to reveal a cool grey dawn, he cooked some breakfast and waited for the sun to rise fully so that he could return to the shore to collect his guests. The sky told him it would be a hot day, ideal for persuading his guests that a day at sea would be perfect.

Impatient for the day to be over, Jonas sailed towards the islands. Attentive to his guests, he found quiet places for them to swim and prepared lunch on a small, deserted beach. He made sure he was always discreet, in the background, but he heard and saw everything. Theirs was not a marriage made in heaven. They squabbled and fought in the pointed way that people of their breeding do, their comments whispered but rapier sharp and their glances filled with poison. He charmed them both with his smile and his knowledge of the islands, all the while fitting their holiday neatly around his business.

As evening began to gather over the coast, Jonas reminded them that they should set sail again in search of dinner. He detected an eagerness to be on shore from Sir John as he turned the Albatross away from the small beach, already enveloped in shadow.

The customs boat was upon them almost before they had turned into the open sea. Two officers boarded the Albatross and Jonas stood quietly at the wheel while they checked his papers.

Sir John, appearing, outraged, from the cabin below, ranted at their impertinence, giving Jonas the perfect opportunity to calm him down, apologise to the customs men and declare they had nothing to hide. All the while, Lady Caroline watched from the stern, her champagne glass twinkling in the half light. It wasn't long before they were allowed to go on their way.

Once again Jonas rowed his guests to shore where they were met by friends. Slightly anxious, he returned to the Albatross, working through new plans in his head. Instinct told him it wasn't safe to make his delivery that night. He cursed inwardly, staring out at the night sky, perfect in its own finery, and scoured the horizon, looking for any sign of the customs boat, unconvinced that they would give in so easily. Normally he would turn his face away from the shore, away from the lights of the town so that he could be at one with the night but tonight he was nervous. He faced the shoreline where diners ate, drinkers chinked glasses and dancers danced close to the water's edge.

He had just begun to allow himself to relax when he noticed movement in the sea close to the shore. Someone was swimming out towards him. Without taking his gaze off the water, he reached down for his binoculars and raised them slowly to his eyes. There was no mistaking the slim figure of Lady Caroline cutting through the still water. Jonas remained where he was, sitting on the deck as Caroline clambered aboard.

She grabbed a towel from the pile on the bench

and approached him warily. The proximity of her in the rich darkness made him catch his breath. Night time suited her. She sat on the bench next to him, pulling the towel through her thick chestnut hair. Jonas remained still, his mind turning over the reason for her being there, grateful that his face was in shadow so that she wouldn't see the confusion in his eyes. He needed to know he could trust her.

She told him that the customs men and the coastguard were with her husband and his party. They were drinking tonight but would be back would be back at first light. Jonas forced himself to listen, mesmerised by her pale skin bathed in moonlight. He needed to think.

"Jonas, you have to go." Her voice, gentle and insistent.
"How did you know?"
"I always knew. But that doesn't matter. Move it now, Jonas. John has a boathouse just round the bay. I have the key. We'll stash it there and then you must come back to the Albatross."

Without another word, she stepped into the rowing boat and waited for Jonas to pass the boxes down. Together they rowed silently round the headland and into Fury Bay where

Sir John's boathouse lay empty. Caroline went ahead to open the doors, leaving a stunned Jonas, his senses on high alert, waiting for the flashing lights of the custom boat to appear. He had never trusted anyone to the extent that he was trusting Caroline at that moment.

She waded back into the water and held the little rowing boat steady as it struggled against the turning tide, while Jonas ran back and forth with the boxes. With the last box in place, they took the boat back around the bay. Just out of sight of the party on the shoreline, Caroline dived into the water and swam back towards them while Jonas turned the boat towards the Albatross.

His heart was beating hard as he flopped on to the deck. He was still laying there when he heard the motor boat. Damn! He screwed his eyes tight shut and waited for the customs men to board.

Caroline stepped aboard with Sir John and watched as the customs officers made a thorough search of the vessel. Jonas remained still. They returned, shaking their heads, apologising to Sir John who having reverted to his position of self-righteous irritation, insisted they return him and Lady Caroline to the shore. Caroline pleaded a headache and retired to her cabin, leaving Jonas alone in the shadows.

He watched the party disembark before he pulled up the anchor and turned the Albatross towards the open sea. Caroline stood behind him, her perfume as sweet as the scent of the night.

©Janis Hall

Night Time

Laying under the stars, waiting for sleep to claim me, I was taken back to my childhood; happy days spent with my grandparents who never seemed to tire of my endless questions.

"Why do cows give us milk, Grandma? How tall is the tallest tree? How do the stars stay up in the sky?"

I was six when I went to live with them and they made my life complete, safe. On the terrible nights when I couldn't sleep, one of them would sit with me and take away the terrors that lurked in the darkness until finally, I came to see the night time as a soft, benign thing, something that healed rather than caused harm.

My parents had both been killed at night, the blackness making it hard for the rescuers to locate them, precious minutes lost while they set up lights bright enough to allow them to search safely through the rubble. They had pulled me from my bed, physically unharmed but the night time had become my nemesis.

A few yards away from me, I heard the snuffling sound of someone crying. Carefully, I picked my way between the sleeping bags, knowing that it would be Henry. He lay on his back, his eyes wide open, too afraid to sleep. Bad things had happened at night to Henry's family.

I stroked his arm gently to let him know I was there and motioned for him to follow me. We placed our sleeping bags side by side and sat together, our arms touching. I wondered how to help unlock the horrors that kept him prisoner.

We spoke quietly of day to day things for a while until Henry whispered, "The night is bad, David. If I close my eyes it will hurt me."

I was taken back in that instant to my grandma's garden. Sitting up, I put an arm around his thin shoulders and started to tell him about the night.

"The earth is like you, Henry. It gets tired. When you've been playing all day, you need to rest. The earth is the same so, she pulls up an enormous soft blanket and it lays it gently over her, covering everything; the trees, the houses, the rivers, the jungle, everything. The blanket helps us rest and helps us heal."

"But it's too dark David. I can't see."

"You can see. Mother Nature's blanket is studded with millions of little lights that never go out. Look. Screw up your eyes and peep out. Can you see them?"

Henry's head tilted back and he looked straight up.

"Can they fall out of the sky?" His voice quavered. I smiled to myself. "No, they won't fall. They've been there for millions of years, looking after us. When she is rested, Mother Earth will gently roll her blanket back and let a new day begin."
"But what if she forgets, David? What if she dies?"

I knew I had to answer very carefully. Henry had seen enough terror in his life.

"Mother Earth won't die, Henry. People die and animals die but Mother Earth will never die. You don't have to worry about that. History tells us that she has always been here, looking after all of us."

"What happens when people die, David?"
I inhaled slowly, knowing that I had to get this right.
"They leave a star to remind us of them. Look up there. Those stars died millions of years ago but they are still shining."
Henry lay back in his sleeping bag, staring at

the bejewelled curtain above him. I sat very still, waiting for the next question. The darkness was now thick, complete. A light breeze relieved the searing heat of the day, scattering the scents of the warm earth.

"Which one's mine?" This drowsy little boy needed an answer. Grandma came to the rescue once more. "They are all yours. Every single little star is gazing down on you, lighting up your path."

Henry wriggled in his sleeping bag and turned to face me.
"I think I will sleep now, David."
I didn't wait for the next question.
"I'll be right here, Henry."

©Janis Hall

Night Time

The sun is asleep, the sky is dark
The time of the owl, not of the lark
The moon up above in all its phases
Whatever its shape, it still amazes.

To some who happen to be superstitious
The thought of night is far from delicious
Each flickering shadow that the eyes can see
Invite such feelings of true mystery.

For those who watch and gaze at stars
And search for planets like Venus and Mars
The vast night sky can be a delight
With Orion's Belt often in sight.

Now, there are some creatures that are
nocturnal
They thrive in darkness that is long not eternal
You may see a glimpse, you may hear a sound
Whatever it is, you know it's around.

In the hours of darkness, even faint sounds are
heard
Though with a loud voice you can hear every
word
And if laughter is raucous and a voice is deep
It may waken those who are fast asleep.

Night Time

When the dawn approaches, the dark fades
away
The end of the night, the start of the day
But if you love the dark, it will return
A reward for those that have this yearn.

© Stuart Foulger

Moonbeam

Emma and Jake were twins. They looked alike, in that they both had fair hair and brown eyes, but Emma's hair was long and straight and Jake's was like a curly mop. Emma was rather shy; Jake would stand up and sing if someone asked him.

They were eight years old and they shared a fear. They didn't like the dark and so couldn't sleep well. Jake would pretend he wasn't nervous but at night he wasn't so confident. Their mother put lamps by their beds which shone all night but it made little difference. In fact, the light caused shadows and the twins imagined awful monsters in their room when really it was just things like the curtains blowing in the breeze from the open window.

Then there were the reflections moving around their room from cars' headlights on the road outside. Their father always read them a nice bedtime story, full of brave knights, princesses and good fairies but as soon as he closed the door it started.

"Jake, what's that black thing moving about?"
"I think it's only the shadow of the curtains but it looks like someone wearing a flowing black cape, doesn't it?"

"Yes, and I don't think it's Superman or a good wizard. It looks evil." Emma hid her face under the bedclothes.

At least they were together, they would have hated to be in separate rooms. They tossed and turned and dozed but didn't really sleep. In the morning when it was daylight, they could have slept properly, but had to go to school.

"Oh, Mum, we can't go today, we are so tired," yawned Emma, trying to eat her cereal.
"Yes, Mum, we can't concentrate on our lessons," mumbled Jake, also yawning.
"If this goes on much longer, I'll have to take you both to the doctor." Their worried Mum looked at their tired eyes and the way they dragged their feet to the door, feeling worn out even before school.

At the weekend Emma was lying in the grass at the bottom of the garden, trying to read but her eyes kept closing. Jake was half-heartedly trying to climb the oak tree but had no energy.

Suddenly a little figure with golden wings and a bright red dress flittered over to Emma. "Hello, do you need my help?" Emma jumped up in a panic and shouted, "Jake, come here." Jake dashed over and stared at the fairy, for that was what she was.

"I don't want to frighten you, but I thought perhaps you had a problem or something the fairies who live nearby could sort out for you."

"Well, thank you very much, but I don't think we need your help," whispered Jake politely, gazing at the lovely fairy.

"You were nodding off, Emma, and it's such a lovely day, I wondered if you were ill."

"Oh, no, it's just that we can't sleep at night; we don't like the dark and so we are tired during the day."

Emma managed to speak but her mouth stayed open as she gazed in wonder.

"Ah, I'm a daytime fairy, but my sister, Moonbeam, looks after the night time. I will have a word with her if you like."

The fairy fluttered a few inches from the ground, showing her bright red dress which was covered in poppy flowers. She wore a garland of bluebells around her head and dangling from her ears were little daisy chains. On her feet, she wore tiny golden slippers decorated with two yellow buttercups.

Jake's mouth managed to say, "You are very pretty." He looked at her in amazement and couldn't take his eyes away.

"Why, thank you, so are you," and her wings

flapped faster and she flew off towards the open field.

Jake and Emma looked at each other and couldn't believe what they had seen and heard. It wasn't possible that they had nodded off and dreamed the beautiful fairy. She was real. You have to believe in fairies, don't you? "I do, I do," whispered Emma.

That night they got ready for bed and their dad read them a lovely story all about Peter Pan and Wendy and of course, Tinkerbell the fairy. They took a lot more interest in Tinkerbell now that they had seen a real fairy for themselves.

Their lamps were left on as usual and the window closed as it was windy that evening. They tried to sleep, they really did, but felt more wide-awake than ever. They talked about the fairy, whose name they didn't know, and wondered about Moonbeam and what she was like.

Suddenly, there was a quiet knock on the window; Jake got up and peered out. A little figure smiled at him and he opened the window.

"Hello, I'm Moonbeam. I knew you wouldn't be asleep because that's why I'm here, isn't it? Sunbright told me all about you." The little figure flew in and sat on the table. Her pretty dress was covered in stars and moons on a midnight blue background. She wore hundreds of tiny crescent moons in her long black hair. On her feet were miniature black boots with shooting stars in silver. She really was very beautiful like Sunbright, but so different.

"So, Sunbright has told me you can't sleep because you are afraid of the dark" smiled Moonbeam.

Emma and Jake both spoke at once "Well, we aren't really frightened but there are so many shadows and everything looks so different and black at night."

"Yes, you're right. All the things you accept by day look different when you can't see them properly. I agree with you there." Moonbeam dangled her legs off the table which caused shadows to appear and it looked as though she had four legs. Emma and Jake laughed.

"That's it, that's what you must do," said Moonbeam. "When you see something which makes you nervous or frightened, but you know it is just an ordinary thing during the day, you must laugh at it. You know it's only the curtain or light or shadows, so just laugh. Your fear will go away and then you'll relax and go to sleep."

"Do you think it will work?" asked Emma. She wanted to ask Moonbeam so many questions about being a fairy but she was shy and her eyes were already beginning to close, although she fought to keep them open.

"Yes, I hope so, come on, try it while I'm here and then I'll know."
"When you are here we can never be afraid," Jake whispered; he didn't want her ever to leave.

Moonbeam laughed. "Well, show me the things which frighten you when I'm not here."
Emma and Jake looked around; they saw the curtain blow in the breeze from the open window. "Okay," said Moonbeam, "now laugh at it, go on."

Emma and Jake burst out laughing. "Ha ha ha!" they both giggled. "Ho ho ho, that's funny!" shouted Jake. How could they be frightened of the dark after they had made fun of it? They couldn't. They laughed, and Moonbeam joined in, and before they knew it they were feeling very sleepy indeed.

They asked Moonbeam if she would stay with them all night. She smiled and said "Well, you

don't need me now but there are other children who do. I will tell them about you, if I may."
"Oh, yes, please do, Moonbeam. Tell them the secret and how well it works."

"I will, and now I must go. Sleep well, Emma and Jake." Moonbeam flew over to the window, turned back to say a final goodbye and disappeared into the night. The twins slept very well and woke up feeling so much better.

"Do you think it was all a dream, Emma?" Jake asked the next morning at breakfast.
"Well, we can't both have had the same dream, can we?" laughed Emma.
Their mother smiled at them and said, "Well you are both looking a lot better today, so if you did dream, it was a good one."
"Mum, we have been cured but you wouldn't believe us if we told you how," laughed Jake.

Their mother asked them what they meant but they wanted to keep Sunbright and Moonbeam their own special secret. They didn't think that grown-ups would understand.

That night when they went to bed, they looked around for Moonbeam but she didn't come knocking at the window again. Emma slipped out of bed to reach for something she saw under the table. What do you think it was? Why, only a tiny crescent moon made of bright silver.

©Jeannie Abbott

Night Time

The Cuttersham village Spring Fair hadn't been too bad, had it? As village fairs go.

An adverse weather forecast had necessitated a last-minute relocation into the village hall, making the programmed events somewhat on the drag. So, it was well past six o'clock when the raffle prizes finally were drawn and the thank-you speeches had heralded the close of business.

To be honest, thought Bob, the only true highlight of the afternoon was his young son's success in the hoop-la. Alfie had won a second-hand die-cast model car, a vintage yellow Lagonda LG6. Its miniature bonnet was already missing when he won it, but what a shame the car had become detached from its base when Alfie dropped his prize minutes later.

"But it's nice to win something isn't it?" offered his mother, Judith. Alfie wasn't impressed.

"Are we really going home at long last?" grunted big sister Louise. She dragged her feet although the others were hurrying now towards the field that served as an overspill parking area. They were well aware of the raindrops becoming heavier as they fell from blackened clouds melded with darkening nightfall.

"Come along, you lot, before we all get drenched!" Bob almost manhandled his wife, the two children and their Dalmatian into the vehicle. "No, Alfie, you can't sit in the front. Your mum sits there. You two get in the back seat with Dotty, and make sure she stays on her blanket."

And then it came. A sudden deluge onto the roof and windscreen of the seven-year old Fiesta. Bob switched the wipers on even before he'd tried the engine.

From the first lightning Alfie counted to six before the thunder came. A few straggling fairgoers, covering their heads with anything they could think of, scurried like ants from under a lifted stone.

"We'll sit it out," said Bob, folding his arms defiantly, "and I'm not going back down the way we came and all those roadworks at Darston. It took ages getting here through that lot. I know a back road we can take if we turn left at that junction, by the diversion sign."

The rain hammered on the roof and was drowning out voices, so they were now shouting.

"Oh Bob, why not go on the main road?"
"It'd take us much longer, that's why. It's an extra seven miles on that road."

Another flash of lightning!

Alfie started counting: "One - two - three - four...it's nearer, Dad, it's getting nearer. You said you had to count..."

"Can we go now?" interrupted Louise, "I've got such a headache."
"We'll go soon, darling." said her mother, trying to ignore her own emerging migraine.

But the rain didn't stop, and soon the Fiesta was one of only half-a-dozen vehicles still left in the field. Tempers frayed, even Dotty was getting restless.

"Right! That's it!"

Bob at last fired up the engine, slammed into gear and drove through the open gate and into the darkness with wheel-spins that ripped the sodden turf into flying mud.

The first couple of miles were scary, to say the least. Incessant downpour, swift rivulets and deep puddles disguising ditches and the edges of the lanes. Headlights on full beam didn't help much round the frequent twists and narrow turns. But with his nose almost touching the water-flushed windscreen Bob peered through and saw what he was looking for. It was lying face down in the mud.

"There it is! The diversion sign. It's blown over. We go left here."

The others hadn't seen it at first, and no-one offered to get out and set it upright. Bob followed the lane for half a mile, and turned at the next junction, alongside a large, mainly derelict barn.

"This must be the one. We go right at the next fork and we'll miss Darston, and the roadworks."
"But the signpost we just passed said Darston is the other way." protested Louise.

Before Bob could respond a pair of lights up ahead made him brake sharply. A tall vehicle with giant wheels approached him at speed then stopped right in front of him, having made no attempt to move over to let the Fiesta pass. Another flash of lightning illuminated the tractor, revealing it to be blue, not black, and showed the driver frantically waving his arms, clearly expecting Bob to reverse. Alfie wasn't counting this time. Bob reluctantly, angrily, wound down his window to hear the man's shouting.

"Go back! It ain't no use you goin' down that way, mate, the ol' Ridebrook bridge is flooded right over. I just been through it, but you ain't gettin' through in that little mini and that's truth!"

Bob hesitated, silently exploring possible responses, but Judith took hold of the situation and very firmly told him to reverse, and to do it now. Seething, he sensibly held his tongue and backed up slowly the way they had come, with the tractor, headlights blazing, advancing bumper to bumper with the Fiesta. At a wider part of the lane the blue monster swerved past him at great speed, covering the little car with mud, vegetation and filthy water. Bob stopped and watched the tractor's red lights rapidly diminishing in his rear-view mirror. Then they were gone.

He considered a three-point, no, a five-point turn. That idea was doomed from the start because the back wheels sank a little into the inevitably hidden ditch. The car wasn't going anywhere. Handbrake on, engine off, in gear. Headlights off. Save the battery. At least he got that right.

"Mum. I've GOT to wee." Louise's voice accentuated her urgency.

"Well, go outside and wee by the door."

"But it's pouring! Can't you see? It's perfectly horrendous!"

"Well, put Dotty's blanket over your head. And be quick."

"I'm not weeing out there with HIM watching."

Alfie defended his virtue: "NOBODY would want to watch YOU weeing, anyway. Yeuk! Gross!"

"Stop that, both of you!" shouted Judith. "Louise, just get on with it."

Dotty whimpered and resisted as her blanket was taken from under her. Then, with a struggle and lots of loudly muttered protests Louise got out of the car and squatted alongside. Immediately the brightest forked lightning struck, somewhere near the old barn, simultaneously with a deafening explosion overhead. Dotty gave an unearthly howl and leaped out of the open door, knocking the screeching Louise headfirst into the ditch. Everyone screamed in unison as the dog vanished at full pelt up the road. Judith scrambled to pull Louise out of the water, twice slipping halfway in herself. Alfie curled in the corner of his seat, crying. Louise's fury betrayed her knowledge of language her parents had not heard from her before.

The escapee howled occasionally in the distance somewhere. As Bob got out of the car, it slid a few more inches towards the ditch. He was sure it couldn't go in much further; there was no danger of that. So, knowing that his family should be safe with Judith, he set off after Dotty, calling her name. In a couple of minutes his calls and the dog's cries were too far away to be heard at all.

Soaked to the skin and not having found the stupid dog, Bob soon reached Ridebrook bridge. The torrent flood was so high he wondered whether this was now the place where the bridge used to be? No possible way through there. Retracing his steps, he eventually came to the spot where he had left his car and family. Neither were there. Maybe he had misjudged the distance; they must be a bit further on. But no, there are the wheel marks in the mud, and look! The dog's blanket lay partially submerged in the ditch. He called out for them, but got no response. Heart beating, he began to run back towards the barn, shouting their names.

As the old barn and the junction came into view he ran past a triangular road sign which simply said 'FLOOD'. The tractor driver must have placed it there to warn that the bridge was impassable. In a few moments, he reached the junction by the barn, and for the first time noticed the old-fashioned, painted signpost. The lane he had just run along was shown as 'BY-ROAD'. To the right, it indicated 'DARSTON ¾'; to the left, 'CUTTERSHAM 2'.

Both of these lanes were blocked by bollards and each of them had a temporary rectangular sign declaring 'ROAD AHEAD CLOSED'.

The rain had eased significantly and the hazy full moon afforded a sinister glow of grey as the clouds began to dissolve. As he stood, bewildered, in the middle of the junction his shoe kicked something that tinkled metallically against the tarmac. He bent over to pick it up and straight away he knew exactly what it was: the tiny yellow bonnet from a die-cast model Lagonda LG6.

©Julian Cope

Night Time (Soul & Heart)

Do you know, I've sometimes asked where you
are, my angelic love?
Do you sit, laughing, on a star up above?
Do you rest up high, in a blossomed tree?
Do you at last, feel unchained and free?
Do you have conversations with every flower?
Do you sprinkle them with a happiness
shower?
Do you ride astride many a silver cloud?
Do you make all other angels proud?
Do you stroke a warm golden sunbeam?
Do you polish rainbows to make them gleam?
Do you blow gentleness on a cooling breeze?
Do you actually stop many a big freeze?

Do you fly over every river and mountain?
Do you throw angel pennies into a fountain?
Do you send that white floating feather?
Do you hold my tears, in rainy weather?
Do you paint the numbers eleven, eleven?
Do you post all beauty down from heaven?
Do you turn the night time light?
Do you shine and make all things bright?
Do you look after your nieces and nephew?
Do you realise how much they love you?

Do you believe it's impossible for us to be
spiritually apart?
Do you know, like I do, that's because we will

be forever entwined; soul and heart.

© Karen J.A. Nunn

Night Time (Just In Time)

Just in the dark moments that we call night,
There's something that makes my sinews
stretch tight.
Then I download high pitched music and I'm
upbeat and alright,
In fact wow, hyper, really way out of sight.

There is a heavy glam-rock band,
Which hails from the most eastern point of
England,
I put on that falsetto sound, which is grand.
Justin, how do you sing, without a ruptured
throat gland?

It may seem peculiar to some,
but with this group, alive I do become.
Feeling magic in my soul and tum,
I smile, thinking of Mr Hawkins wriggly bum.

The glitzy, skimpy, colourful gear,
Reminds me to be full of cheeky cheer.
Oh, please hurry on, back to Claremont Pier,
so folks can watch and gleefully hear,
I know you'll be received greatly, that's clear.

Their music makes many a foot tap,
That is great for Lowestoft Town; to ensure it is
placed firmly on the map.

Night Time

So nightly, The Darkness will deliver me a
thrill,
As I tune into their songs, I actually shrill.

Dear Justin, kindly be my knight in spandex,
shining armour,
If only in my dreams, at night-time, bring on
more of your amour.
Because, like many a feeling, from above,
I so believe in a thing called love.

© Karen J.A. Nunn

Late Night Run

No one knows about my late-night jogs at three in the morning. My friends and especially my family would only tell me how crazy I am; running around in the freezing cold, in the dead of the night with potential thugs, thieves and murderers lurking in the shadows around every corner. They'd worry more because I'm a woman: a weak, vulnerable and delicate flower, apparently. Little do they and my husband know how good I've become at hiding things.

My body clock stirs me awake and my immediate instinct is to roll away from being my husband's big spoon and catch the numbers glowing a soft red on the alarm clock. 2:32am. That's the easy bit done. Now comes the hard part.

I glance at my sleeping spouse while lifting the corner of the duvet cover ever so slightly, sliding one leg out and planting my bare foot on the carpet. I check to see if I moved too much to wake him. I can hear him breathe and he still hasn't noticed the absence of my embrace. I slowly drag my other leg out of the bed to join the other one on the floor before standing up and placing the duvet cover back where it was. I don't want to lose too much heat to wake him up. Wading through the darkness, I snap my focus between my husband and the door. It practically feels like I'm creeping past a sleeping dragon. My hand pats along the smooth wall until I feel a wooden surface, sliding my hand down to the door handle to my right. I take a deep breath and push it down, cringing at the creak as I pull the door open.

A snore.

My body stiffens as I lock my eyes on my rousing husband. Oh God, he's moving! Please don't turn around! He moans and mumbles incoherently, snuggling a little bit before he's still once more. I don't escape right away; I want to make sure he's definitely asleep. Those few seconds of waiting are torture. Nothing happens. Still nothing. He's not moving anymore. Now I can slip out of the bedroom and quietly shut the door behind me.

I pick up the pace a little, power walking across the landing without waking our two children, and down the stairs straight towards the laundry room.

It's a good thing I'm the only person who really uses this place since I'm the only one with the capacity to operate a washing machine. I click the light switch on and the room blinds me for a few seconds. Once my eyes adjust to its brightness, I turn to the white chest of drawers next to the washing machine and jerk the middle drawer open, raising the many coloured towels to grab some elasticated material. Changing in the laundry room doesn't sound as awkward as most people think; clothes are washed here after all. I remove my violet night dress and tug my yellow, long sleeved sports shirt and three-quarter white sports leggings on myself before snatching a hairband from the top of the washing machine and turning off the light.

I tie my shoulder length, brown hair into a bun down the darkened hallway towards the front door. Once I freed both my hands, I slip my feet into my running trainers before grabbing the keys from the wall hook and opening the door.

Fresh air hits my face followed by the security light beaming above me. With a tentative click of the lock and shutting the door, I can almost imagine a choir of angels singing praises of my successful attempt of escape; the light shining down on me helps create that impression. But now for the part I've been waiting for; I push the keys down my pocket, jog out of the light and into the darkness of this familiar road. The stones crunch underneath my feet as I leave the driveway and turn right.

The pitch-blackness reminds me of the government's attempt to save money by turning off the street lamps to the smaller roads. A lot of people complained that it would give burglars and unscrupulous individuals more opportunities to commit their crimes during the night. It makes it easier for them to conceal. I kind of agree but then aren't we hiding things during the day, too? Everyone wears their own masks to hide true intentions and emotions they think it is forbidden to feel, especially in front of society.

I turn a corner to a gravel path leading into the woods not too far from where I live. For some reason, the lamp posts there are still lit with an orange glow so I can see my feeble condensation expire with each breath I take. Apart from my footsteps, the gentle breeze rustling the trees and the very occasional bark from foxes that sounds more like someone yelping in pain, the place is quiet. The silver moon and twinkling stars are the only visible things in the black sky when I look up. I can see why some people would call that romantic and definitely mysterious. They're so vast and far away and yet we succeeded in exploring it in our rockets.

I can only imagine how it must have felt to step outside. The moon would probably have been peaceful too, with nothing and no one for miles around. And the sight of Earth from where those astronauts stood must have been breathtaking; the blue and green planet just there, like the moon is from here.

As much as I would love to spend time thinking about space, I have to face forward or I'll trip over a stone or something. I follow the path around to the left and come to a familiar part of the street I've been down before on my previous runs.

I leave the whistling woods behind and head towards a large, open playing field where dog-walkers, pram pushers, cyclists and pedestrians normally mind their own business. Most people find it eerily strange and scary for places full of people during the day to be empty. I suppose this is what they call the uncanny. We're told as kids to be home before dark or scary monsters would haunt us but there's nothing here save for a playground I'm approaching.

Maybe the lack of people and the emptiness is what makes them feel uncomfortable; we are social creatures after all, and working in groups and teams is practically ingrained into our heads nowadays. The problem is no one seems to have the time to sit and reflect on things by themselves. I guess I can understand the appeal of not being alone but to deny ourselves some time in our own worlds without anyone else influencing us is just sad.

We're not allowed to be ourselves during the day. That's why I like these late-night runs; I can ramble about this sort of stuff and go off on different tangents without anyone else's expectations.

Of course, all good things must come to an end.

I find my pitch-black road again and by some miracle, locate my house. The security light beams once more as my fingers stroke every key until I find the one that unlocks the front door. I slip into the house slowly with as much stealth as I can muster, hanging the keys back onto the hook and using my toes as leverage to remove my trainers.

I tip-toe down the hallway towards the laundry room where my running clothes are thrown into the washing machine and my night dress is back on as it should be.

I climb the stairs, searching for the places on

the steps where no creaks can be heard with my bare feet. Reaching the top without incident, I creep down the hallway in hopes of not waking the kids up. I let out a small sigh of relief as I reach the bedroom door. Pushing the handle as soft as I possibly can, I enter the room with timid steps.

As soon as I lock eyes on my husband, I press the door shut with a soft click with gritted teeth. I glance to find he's moved slightly but still asleep. Or maybe he's noticed but was too tired to actually think I'd go beyond the front door. Either way, I carefully lift the duvet cover and slide into the bed before placing it down. I don't want to trip at the last hurdle and wake him up because he felt a cold breeze. I take my role as the big spoon again and drape an arm over my sleeping spouse as I finally close my eyes. If he happens to ask where I've gone, I could always tell him I was getting a glass of water from downstairs. But that's only if he asks me in the morning.

©Natasha Mickleburgh

The Sounds of the Night

The fox bark sounds more like a yelp.
or the sound of someone screeching: HELP

Muntjacs bark a deep throated sound
you can always tell when they are around.

Owls: we all now go, tweet twoo.
but with some it's more like a meow.

The farmer's cattle stand mooing low
the bull sometimes gives a bellow.

Horses nicker and neigh
as they stand and eat their hay.

In the distance, a car zooms along
the driver probably singing a song.

His radio loud to the sound of boom booms,
he drives past the sleeping house: zoom.

Tractors humming as the farmers fight
to harvest their crops, lights shinning bright.

The house creaks as it settles for the night
sometimes a loud crack but it's alright.

Just the wood cooling down,
but it can be an unnerving sound.

Night Time

The country is not a quiet place
life carries on at the same pace.

It's not quiet. The sounds never cease.
So don't move there for some peace

But the dark and the night sky
more stars than we ever knew, oh my.

Say, on a cool clear night in May
with no other light to get in the way,

they are a wonder to behold
just stand and look in the night, so cold.

©Diana Bettinson 2017

Night Time

Joseph was six years old. He wasn't like all his friends who hated bedtime, he loved going to bed. He looked forward to it and loved the really dark and windy nights. He didn't like it when the nights were lighter and he fell asleep before he could see all his shadow friends on his bedroom walls and ceiling. Joseph did not have any brothers or sisters but he did have lots of imaginary friends. He didn't tell anyone about these friends, they were special and different.

He also loved his cuddly black toy dog, called Monty. He had been given Monty when he was two years old, he was as big as Joseph then. His dad named him Monty, and Monty it had stayed. Joseph talked to him about his imaginary friends because he knew Monty wouldn't tell anyone, it was their secret.

It was a November day; it had been cold, wet and dull. Six o'clock struck from the hall clock. Joseph was just finishing his tea. He looked out of the window; tonight, all my friends will come to see me, it made him feel very happy.

The hall clock was now striking 7pm and Joseph's mum was tucking him up in his cosy bed.

"Don't pull the curtains," Joseph said

Mum kissed him goodnight, turned out the light, and closed the door.

He waited. The room was very dark, there was no moon tonight, this meant that some of his friends may not come to see him. Suddenly Stickman appeared. He was dancing in the wind on Joseph's ceiling.

"Hello," said Joseph. Stickman waved to him and danced around some more. Joseph got out of bed quietly, and looked out of the window. It had started to rain.

Stickman was looking at Joseph and waving his arms in the direction of the far wall in his bedroom, and there was Night Goblin with a twiggy hat and long-branch like body. He was smiling.

The trees outside the window were blowing around violently and the rain was pouring down. Stickman seemed to be in a dancing craze, waving his arms everywhere. Joseph danced along with him. Night Goblin was swaying from side to side. It was a party without music. Joseph got Monty and made him start dancing along with them saying, "Come along, Monty, let's have some fun!"

After about half an hour the rain stopped and the wind died down. Stickman and Night

Goblin stopped dancing and swaying and were calm. Joseph got back into bed with Monty. He asked Night Goblin what he had been doing that day. Night Goblin gently swayed; Joseph thought he must have had a happy day.

He then started to tell, in great detail, what he had been doing all day. He wondered why Night Goblin just nodded in a way that made Joseph feel very sleepy.

Stickman was disappearing from the ceiling stick by stick, first his arms and legs, then his whole body disappeared into the shadows. The room was very dark now, the evil black night clouds had taken away his friends. Joseph closed his eyes, just as Moonie-Man popped out from behind a cloud. Joseph caught a glimpse of him smiling goodnight before he fell asleep.

When his mum came up to check he was asleep, all was quiet. Night Goblin was still swaying on the far wall watching over Joseph. Mum walked across the bedroom and drew the curtains; Night Goblin disappeared into the night.

The bedroom was now very dark indeed. Joseph and Monty were sleeping peacefully. The slow rattle of Joseph's steady breath filled the air and in Joseph's head dreams were beginning to take shape. Suddenly he jumped up awake, startled, he couldn't see anything. Darkness crept along the room like monsters, snarling, growling, clawing at the walls, these weren't Joseph's friends, they were night time monsters!

Where were his beloved Stickman, Night Goblin and Moonie-man when he needed their protection? Joseph was so frightened, terrified in fact.

"H-h-hello," he stuttered "I'm J-Joseph, WHY ARE YOU HERE!"
"We are the creatures of the night!" they shouted back

Joseph gulped, he glanced over the top of his duvet. The monsters were closing in, it was so, so dark. Where are my friends? he thought. He felt like crying, maybe his friends were afraid to come and help him. He rolled over in bed to hide under his duvet; he looked towards the window,

"THE CURTAINS ARE CLOSED!" he screamed. "Stickman, Night Goblin, Moonie-Man, why are they closed?" Of course, there was no answer and the room seemed darker still.

He had to get to the window and open the curtains. He had to be brave. He pushed back the duvet very gently, swung his legs round feeling for the floor with his feet, his heart was pounding and he felt very hot.

"Be brave, be brave," he kept saying to himself. Suddenly he made a dash for the window, but oops! He fell over a book he had left lying on the floor. He lay there for what seemed like ages, he could feel the night monsters' breath on his neck.

"GO AWAY!" he shouted, scrabbling around, picking himself up. He had no idea if he was heading in the right direction for the window but he had to open the curtains, he took a chance.

He held his hands out in front of him to feel for the curtains and there they were. He flung them back in a flurry of fear. The moonlight from Moonie-Man filled his bedroom and the night monsters instantly disappeared!

"Thank you, thank you, Moonie-Man," Joseph said. Stickman was once more waving and Night Goblin was swaying in his usual way, all was calm at last.

Joseph was exhausted, he had battled the night

monsters and won, thanks to his friends. As he climbed back into bed, Mum appeared in the doorway of his room.

"Are you ok, Joseph, I heard you shouting. Were you having a bad dream?"
"I'm alright," he said shakily, "I will tell you all about it in the morning. Please leave the curtains open I like to see the moon." And with that he fell asleep instantly.

***

The winter sun was shining through Joseph's window when he woke up the next morning. His friends were nowhere to be seen. He jumped out of bed and looked out of the window. The garden looked the same as always. He grabbed Monty from the bed and said, "We did it, we did it, we battled the night monsters and won. Hooray, hooray, tonight when my friends come we will have another dancing party. I will never be afraid of the night monsters again."

His mum didn't mention his dream, so Joseph didn't say anything either. He decided to write a story about his night friends and how they had all won the fight with the night monsters. He was so proud of himself and his friends.

He decided that Night Time was exciting,

everything was different, a whole new world where battles could be fought and won! It was just great to be six!

© Marion Rainbird

Night time

At night I like to sit and stare,
through the window in the open air,
I watch the insects and the mice,
roaming wild and free - wouldn't that be nice?
The wind on my face, whistling by my ears,
many sounds of the evening, forget all my
fears.
The fish in the pond, all asleep in a dream,
Thinking of springtime and swimming in a
stream.
The darkness falls but through the gleaming
moonlight,
I see the rabbits playing, their elegant ears
upright,
listening for foxes, I guess, or wolves, or
bigger,
who knows what is out there, anything, I
figure.
You see, I'm not too sure, as I'm a house cat by
day.
My owners keep me safe, warm and fed, I am
not a stray.
I'm grateful for my bed, for my toys and my
treats,
but I will forever wonder, how it feels on the
streets.
To explore the world in the magnificent night,
seeing the flowers up close, their colours so
bright.

Night Time

But what if it's scary? In the dark and the cold,
no home to run back to, I would be frightened
not bold.
Maybe it's not such a wonderful plan,
I run up the stairs as fast as I can.

At night, I like to sit and stare,
At my wonderful sleeping humans in their bed
(which I share).
All safe and warm and cosy and snug.
No sign of the scary night time, not even a bug!
Under the duvet I sneak with a purr,
give my humans a mouthful of my soft ginger
fur.
They stroke me and tell me I am a good cat,
oh, I'm so glad I'm inside at night, that's a fact!

©Kate Walsh

Dear Reader
If you have enjoyed reading this book, please
leave us a review on Amazon.
Thank you.

The Authors

Aisha Khalaf

Aisha was born in South America and moved with her parents to the UK at the age of 10. She relocated from Oxford to Lowestoft about twenty years ago. Once she retired from her legal practice she took up writing full time. Combining her love of history with the theories on the life of Tutankhamun, Aisha recently published her first historical fiction Tutankhamum – He is Born, the first of her trilogy under the pen name of ADP Sorisi.

Aisha enjoys the theatre, reading, swimming, walking, good food and dear friends when her writing allows. She is a mother of four with four granddaughters.
https://www.facebook.com/ADP-Sorisi-187852201705443/

Claire Walker

Claire Walker has been an aspiring author for many years and believes that her recent move from Manchester to beautiful Suffolk has really fired her imagination.

She enjoys walking on the beach and daydreaming about gorgeous heroes for the best-selling romance novel she is one day going to write. A Room for the Night is her first published work.

Claire is a member of the Waveney Author Group.

Cara Mickleburgh

Cara lives and works in the (sometimes) sunny town of Lowestoft. She mainly spends her time taking care of her pets that include her two dogs.

Cara enjoys reading and writing about fantastic and whimsical things that might just be hiding around the corner.

When no one is in ear shot, she likes to sing off-key to movie sound tracks.

Diana Bettinson

Diana has always enjoyed writing stories and poems. She has completed one book for older children and is working on an adult novel.

There is going to be a book about her horse who was called Nicholas.

She hopes you enjoy the poem and that the

anthology raises a lot of money for Alzheimer's Research.

You can follow Diana at

https://www.facebook.com/Diana-Bettinson-Author-page-158069648021521/

Jeannie Abbott

Jeannie Abbott has lived in Suffolk for twelve years, originating from Stockport, near Manchester.

She never had a lot of time to write when working full-time as a freelance secretary, but since retiring enjoys scribbling for pleasure.

Writing for children and quirky, silly stories are her favourites. Jeannie also runs two free writing groups from Woodbridge Library.

Karen J.A. Nunn

Karen J.A. Nunn enjoys writing many genres, as an author she's committed to inking out of her comfort zones.

In this, her third anthology, she has entered two very diverse pieces being extremely different from her previous published writings.

She longs for Alzheimer's to be history. Karen continues putting pen to paper as a legacy for her wonderful grandchildren and in memory of her late daughter.

Natasha Mickleburgh

When Natasha isn't working at a DIY store far from her hometown of Lowestoft, she's turning odd socks into sock dolls, composing songs, singing when she thinks no one else is around, and writing stories.

This is the first time she has participated in a writing competition and she hopes to enter more in the future.

Marion Rainbird

Marion was born an only child in Stepney, East London in March 1948. She attended school in East Ham (Newham), where she enjoyed English and Music throughout her school life.

She is discovering story writing for children in her retirement.

Marion lives in Beccles, is married to Tony, and has two children Lisa and Andrew, and one granddaughter, Kitty-Jean.

N. A. Dench

N. A. Dench is a Suffolk writer who loves to read and explore new things. He spends his time writing website content for a variety of different clients as well as working on his first novel.

One of his many interests is exploring the great Suffolk coastline.

MJ Wells

Born in Lowestoft, MJ has always enjoyed writing, though never considered herself as a writer.

With less freedom over the last few years due to health issues, she has focused more on this, writing poems and odes, and with the support of her wonderful husband and friends, is currently working on a book to make people smile.

MJ is a member of the Waveney Author Group.

Pat Casselden

Pat has been writing short stories and poetry for several years for her own enjoyment. and has been pleased to have entries in the anthologies Dreaming on Paper and View of the Sea, both raising money for Alzheimer's Research UK.

This time she was thrilled to be chosen as a winner for her story Night Time Terror. Pat looks forward to seeing it in this new anthology, continuing to raise money for this very worthy cause.

Julian Cope

Julian Cope moved to Suffolk in 1982 and loves it. A wartime baby in the Midlands, he has been a trolleybus conductor, banker (hated that), community developer, restaurateur, staff trainer, and football referee, (still going after 48 seasons).

In retirement, he has caught the writing bug. This is his debut publication. There will be more; you ain't seen nuffin' yet!

Janis Hall

A love of stories and story-telling inspire Janis to write. She belongs to a small writing group and gets inspiration from many things but finds people the most fascinating.

A conversation overheard, a glance between

two strangers, it's all grist to the mill.

Stuart Foulger

This is his second poem to be published. He is self-employed and a former district and town councillor.

Stuart lives in Beccles and lived previously in Lowestoft and Los Angeles. He is planning to write a book soon.

Rosalyn Whitfield

Rosalyn has lived in Hertfordshire with her husband for over twenty years. For the last five years they have shared their life with a White Russian cat, named Cartier.

Rosalyn has been a volunteer with the local hospital for 16 years and also runs craft groups, meditation evenings, which she writes herself. She enjoys reading and, of course, writing.

Kate Walsh

Devoting the week to her role as communications manager, Kate is no stranger to writing, but is normally creating strategies or policies, not utilising her devotion to all things fiction.

Spending her spare time playing football for Luton Town, Kate has found dedicating time to writing difficult but aspires to change this once she hangs up her boots for good!

Kate can be found on Twitter @KCWalshy

Jo Wilde, editor

Jo was born in Bradford, slightly too young to be a boomer, and quite a lot too old to be a millennial. Born in Bradford, she has lived in Lowestoft for thirty-five years, apart from a brief but intense affair with York in the early 90s.

She works as a librarian, editor, publisher, designer, researcher...in fact, whatever people will pay her to do, as long as it involves books in some way.

She currently has more books than cats, but will admit to probably having too many of both.

https://www.facebook.com/editEdit-1565473480414442/
@jowilde_editor

Anthologies

This book, Night Time, is the fourth book created specifically to raise money for Alzheimer's Research UK.

The first is a chain book, with each chapter being written by a different author, who take the collective name of Caterina Longtail. It tells the story of a charming cat and her adventures.

Subsequently, a second book grew out of a seed of an idea planted at a writers' weekend. Dreaming on Paper is a book of short stories by local creative writers, and although the brief – to set a story around a Creative Writing workshop – is a fairly specific one, there is a variety and breadth to the stories which ensures something to interest and entertain any reader.

View of the Sea, the second anthology, contains the winning entries from the East Anglian Festival of Culture's second writing competition, and is a diverse showcase of some of the best in creative writing.

Little Kitty the Cat Burglar
ISBN-13: 9780993169076

Dreaming on Paper
ISBN: 9780995484429

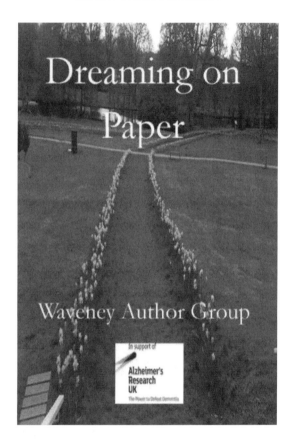

View of the Sea
ISBN: 978-0995484467

VIEW
OF THE
SEA
C. Scape

Printed in Great Britain
by Amazon